For Baby Megan, with love

Designed by Louise Millar

Printed and bound in Belgium by Proost
for the publishers Piccadilly Press Ltd.,
5 Castle Road, London NW1 8PR

ISBN: 1 85340 654 6 paperback
1 85340 659 7 hardback

3 5 7 9 10 8 6 4

Set in Bembo 30pt

A catalogue record for this book is available from the British Library

Other books in the TOFFEE series:

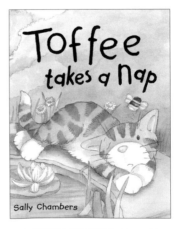

TOFFEE IN TROUBLE
ISBN: 1 85340 594 9 (p/b)

TOFFEE TAKES A NAP
ISBN: 1 85340 617 1 (p/b)

*Sally Chambers lives in Hayes, Kent. She has written and illustrated a number of
picture books. BARTY'S SCARF and BARTY'S KETCHUP CATASTROPHE,
about an independent-thinking sheep, are also published by Piccadilly Press.*

Toffee's new friend

Sally Chambers

Piccadilly Press • London

Toffee was
very excited.
There was a
removal van
next door!

New neighbours!
What would they be like?

So many things
came out of the van.
Tables and chairs,
beds and lamps
and bookshelves.
Box after box . . .
after box.

The next day Toffee spotted something funny under the garden gate.

That evening she saw something funny through the window.

The day after that she saw the
cat-flap move!

And the day after that Toffee came down
to breakfast to find . . .

A kitten . . .
and in her kitchen too!

She frightened it away.

Toffee didn't want the kitten
in her kitchen.

She went to her favourite spot
to think, swishing her tail.

Pat!
Pat!
Pat!
It was the kitten.

Toffee felt
crosser than ever.

"I'll hide in the leaves under the old apple tree," thought Toffee.

"The kitten won't find me there."

But . . .

The kitten fell
into the
soft leaves . . .

right on top
of Toffee!

The wind whirled the leaves into the air.
Toffee pounced and
leaped at them.

So did the kitten!

They both loved
chasing the
leaves.

It was a wonderful game.

Toffee and the kitten had so much fun playing together.

Toffee decided she liked her new neighbour after all.

But the kitten wasn't the only
new neighbour . . .